Words to Know Before You Read

about

do

how

like

more

yes

you

www.rourkepublishing.com

Edited by Luana K. Mitten
Illustrated by Anita DuFalla
Art Direction and Page Layout by Renee Brady

Library of Congress Cataloging-in-Publication Data

Greve, Meg
It's Broken! / Meg Greve.
  p. cm. -- (Little Birdie Books)
ISBN 978-1-61741-806-8 (hard cover) (alk. paper)
ISBN 978-1-61236-010-2 (soft cover)
Library of Congress Control Number: 2011924658

Rourke Publishing
Printed in the United States of America, North Mankato, Minnesota
060711
060711CL

www.rourkepublishing.com - rourke@rourkepublishing.com
Post Office Box 643328 Vero Beach, Florida 32964

IT's Broken!

By Meg Greve

Illustrated by Anita DuFalla

I like jumping,
yes I do.

4

I like jumping,
how about you?

I like bouncing,
yes I do.

I like bouncing,
how about you?

"No more jumping.
No more bouncing!"
yelled Mom.

9

I like hopping,
yes I do.

I like hopping,
how about you? 11

I like leaping,
yes I do.

12

I like leaping,
how about you?

"No more hopping.
No more leaping!"
yelled Mom.

We like jumping, bouncing, leaping, and hopping!

16

Oh no, too high!

I like sitting, yes I do. I'll stay sitting, how about you?

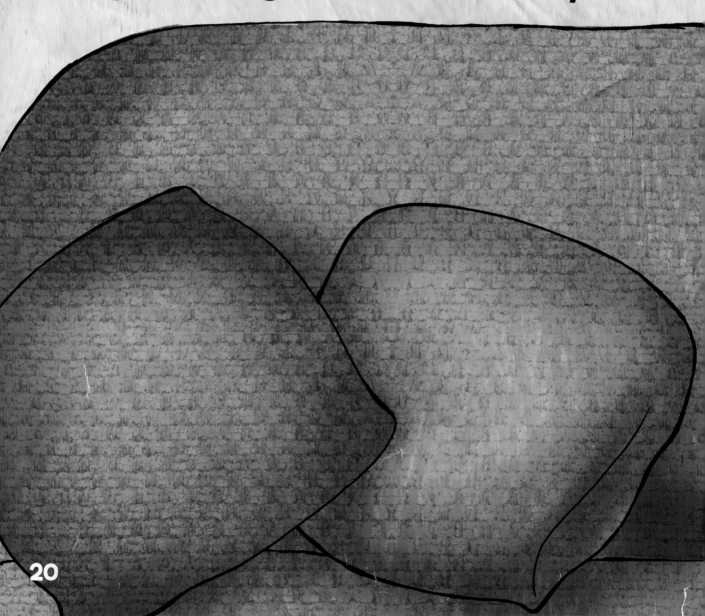

After Reading Activities

You and the Story...

Have you ever bounced on your bed?

Did you get in trouble?

What other games could you play inside?

Words You Know Now...

On a piece of paper, write a word that rhymes with each of the words you know now.

about	more
do	yes
how	you
like	

You Could... Invite a Friend Over to Play Inside Games

- Create a list of games you can play inside.

- What do you need to play these games?

- Where will you play these games?

- Who will you invite to play with you?

About the Author

Meg Greve lives in Chicago with her husband, daughter, and son. Her son loves to jump, bounce, leap, and hop on his bed. Sometimes Meg does too!

About the Illustrator

Acclaimed for its versatility in style, Anita DuFalla's work has appeared in many educational books, newspaper articles, and business advertisements and on numerous posters, book and magazine covers, and even giftwraps. Anita's passion for pattern is evident in both her artwork and her collection of 400 patterned tights. She lives in the Friendship neighborhood of Pittsburgh, Pennsylvania with her son, Lucas.